Title: *Mines, Theirs, Our Love*
Subtitle: *Werewolf Shifter Threesome MFM Romance Story*

From the Author:
Thank you for purchasing this book.

Table of Contents

Mines, Theirs, Our Love
Description

Candace is not what most people call popular with men. She spends most of her time working as a senior designer at a notable fashion company, but everything changes when she bumps into Marlon, to whom there is instant attraction. Candace is later paired to work with the contracted architect but resists his advances due to job-related regulations.

Stood up by her friend, Paul, the owner of a bar assists Candace after she becomes too drunk to take care of herself. This escalates into an act Candace regrets, fleeing the scene the following morning.

With a new outlook, Candace gives in to Marlon's advances and is stunned to find out how closely he is connected to Paul. However, the three have good chemistry and are having a pleasant time when they are interrupted by intruders. As Marlon and Paul defend her, Candace is shocked to discover that the two men have an even deeper connection. Can she accept what they offer or would she run from the discovery?

Chapter 1

A smile spread across Candace's face right before her eyelids fluttered open. Then it all rushed to her, and she sprang from her bed in a rush. She grabbed her phone from the nightstand near her bed, then rushed to the bathroom of her single room apartment. She didn't need the phone to tell her the time, though. The risen sun was enough to inform her she was late.

"I am so dead," Candace mumbled, splattering toothpaste all over the sink.

Candace had been working with her company for five years, long enough for her to know that her boss did not condone tardiness. The first time she was late, she was still an assistant and the speech she received from her then supervisor was enough for her to ensure she was never late again. Until now.

Within a minute, Candace was out of the bathroom, her hair falling to her face in its drenched state.

It was times like those it thrilled her to be living in an apartment smaller than her childhood bedroom. Everything she needed for a speedy departure was well within reach.

Candace pulled on her trousers without ironing them. Luckily it was a stretched material, so the wrinkles didn't look too pronounced. Her blouse, however, was a different story, so Candace settled for a simple t-shirt tucked inside her trousers. It fashioned well with the white sneakers she wore.

Usually, she wore makeup, keeping it light, but today she opted out of it completely, settling for a small gold stud to accessorize her outfit.

Candace was already outside her apartment when she remembered the folders and samples she had brought home with her the day before. Scrabbling back into her apartment to retrieve them and released her first sigh of the day. The first of many.

The bus she took every morning to work had already passed, and the next one was fifteen minutes away. Candace couldn't wait that long, so she opted for a taxi instead, spending the money she had catered for her lunch for the ride to work.

It was the peak of the morning rush and traffic was backed up on all the streets. Drivers honked their horns loudly even though the act had no effect. Vehicles had nowhere to go.

"Just drop me off here," Candace said, as she stuffed a clump of cash into the driver's hand. The elderly man widened his eyes as she sprang from his car, folders in hand.

Candace zoomed across veterans' park to emerge on the intersecting street with sweat trickling down the side of her face. She was breathless, which only served as a reminder of how out of shape she was. Going to the gym was always delayed when she had extended workdays, and Candace almost always had an overflowing workload. After a while, she gave up on the gym completely.

Releasing a loud breath as her work building came into view, Candace pushed through the pain of her constricting lungs and heavy feet to shorten the distance to the building. A smile was on her face as she peered through the glass, noticing several of her coworkers entering the elevator. She should have kept her eyes on her path. If she did, she wouldn't have collided, falling to the ground with all her contents.

"Are you ok?" From where she sat on the concrete, Candace raised her gray eyes to meet the striking green ones of a tall but handsome man. He held out his hand to help her to her feet, but she couldn't get past his light blonde hair and pronounced jawline. The man had a smile drawn across his lips that was not seductive, yet a sensation tickled Candace's center. "Maybe I should call an ambulance."

Shaking her head out of her daze, Candace accepted the hand she was offered. "No, no, I'm fine," she announced, ignoring the ache in her ass. "I'm sorry I didn't see you there. Are you ok?"

The man chuckled, and it made his features even more attractive. "You're the one that fell, but you're worried about me?" He tilted his head. "What's your name?"

Candace opened her mouth, but her name got caught in her throat. Having this man so close to her was rattling her insides. "Candace. My name is Candace."

"Well, Candace, you sure do have a lot of tools," the stranger said, teasing in his voice.

Candace followed his eyes to where her belongings scattered around them; papers, fabric, and the tools needed to strip them.

"Oh," she gasped and dropped to her knees to retrieve the materials. "These are for work."

The stranger was also helping her to pick up her stuff. "I take it you work in the fashion industry."

Candace tilted her head, her mind blown. "How did you guess?"

The man stood tall now, his features even more handsome, with the sun highlighting them. "Well. For one, those papers have dress designs and we're standing in the middle of the fashion district."

"Oh," Candace said, her face becoming flushed. It was then she remembered the reason she bumped into this man in the first place. Candace edged toward her office building. "I'm sorry I have to go. Thank you for everything," she yelled behind her as the distance between them grew wider.

Just before the long hand on the clock in the lobby showed 9:00 am, Candace placed her ID card against the card reader. With a little luck and a whole lot of endurance, she made it just in time.

Tossing the documents onto the desk in her small office, Candace logged on to her computer, getting ready for the long hours ahead. She had not even finished prepping when the office phone rang. Candace answered the phone with an enthusiasm that deflated when she heard her boss' voice.

"Miss Bartholomew," the woman said in a sharp tone. "I need you in my office now."

The phone cut off before Candace even had a chance to respond. Instead of leaving immediately, she sank into her chair, using the moment to recuperate and frame her mind for the encounter.

"Candace, you're here," Sarah Andrews announced after Candace walked into her office. "Allow me to introduce Marlon Henson. Marlon is the architect designing our showroom."

The woman then addressed the man, staring at Candace with striking green eyes. "Marlon, this is Candace Bartholomew. She'll be your consultation for this project."

Candace was still enthralled by the stranger, a stranger she ran into on the streets not too long ago, when her boss' words finally sank in. "You want me to what?" She forced her eyes away from the third occupant, his presence overpowering even with her boss' commanding eyes piercing her.

"I want you to be his consultation for this project. We have a certain requirement as designers and I'm putting you in charge of keeping him in the know." Sarah's voice was firm, which hinted at a finality.

Still, Candace had to at least try. She was swamped enough at it was. Adding another task to her day would deprive her of even more sleep. "Ms. Andrew. I am already strained. Maybe one of the junior assistants can take this task. I know they would be happy for the opportunity."

"There is no way I can give this responsibility to a junior designer." Sarah's eyes were intense. "This room would be with us for a long time and I don't think they can help capture the idea of our brand. Not the way you can."

Sarah had a point. The company would be stuck with the showroom even if the designers did a poor job. It was best to let someone much more capable handle it. Although she didn't understand why it should be her. Sarah was in a much better position to deal with the design. She was the boss, after all. "I understand that, but it's just that I already have so much work on my schedule. I can't possibly fit something else."

Sarah looked at Candace with narrowed eyes, annoyed that she was doing this in front of the company, but if Sarah had considered informing her beforehand, they would have had the conversation then.

"I don't care what you do. You can give one of the others a lesser important project for all I care, but you *are* handling this." There was irritation in her voice as she spoke now, and Candace knew better than to aggravate her any further.

"Yes, ma'am," she complied with her hands in her lap and her head slightly low. "I'll see to it."

"Great." The single word was one of dismissal, and Candace nodded to her new partner before leaving the office.

As she walked out, Candace heard her boss giving Marlon his last instructions and Candace's contact information. She pushed out her lips as creases formed on her forehead. With this added project, Candace was not going to get any sleep.

Chapter 2

"Ok, so here is closest to the window and should be able to fit at least five mannequins. We want to be able to fit five outfits from the same line." Candace flicked through the papers on her desk, seemingly searching for something. "This display is the most important since it gets clients inside the building." She released a heavy sigh and slammed the folder closed. "I must have left the samples in my office. If you can give me a minute." She pushed herself from the leather chair in the conference room. "It will only take a minute."

"But unnecessary." Marlon held her in place, the spot where he clung to her wrist tingling from his touch. "I understand completely. Please." He released her hand and pointed to the chair. "Let's continue."

Candace was hesitant, more because of the strange sensation overwhelming her now than the possibility of her needs being misunderstood. Still, she sat, her eyes taking in everything other than Marlon's.

"So I was thinking about rising this area at the entrance." One eyebrow was raised as Marlon highlighted the area in the diagram on the tablet. "Maybe I'll layer it like steps so mannequins can be displayed on each layer."

Candace's eyes were wide now. She couldn't believe how in-tune with displays this architect was. With him spearheading the display room, her presence was unnecessary. "And it would also highlight the outfits displayed there. That's a great idea."

Marlon smiled, and it tugged at Candace's heart. *Why is he so sexy?* At that moment, all she wanted was to be closer to him, to feel the warmth of his body engulfing her. With her throat suddenly dry, Candace pushed away from the striking man at her side, pushing strands of loose, straight blonde hair behind her ears. It was an act that found Marlon's attention and the amusement in his eyes was unwaveringly apparent.

When it came to men, Candace was vastly inexperienced. She was drawn to Marlon in a way that was unfamiliar, yet she did not know how to act. The knowledge of her attraction made her even more awkward and her clumsiness peered through. With no genuine experience with men, at the age of thirty, she felt like an outcast, doomed to spend her days at her desk completing endless tasks.

Burying her emotions behind her work, Candace continued with her consultation. "For every line, we usually come out with beachwear, so I was thinking of dedicating an entire section to this."

Marlon stared at the preliminary designs. "I think building this area," he pointed to the tablet. "Surrounding it with glass so that the sand wouldn't get on everything."

"Sand?" Candace tilted her head.

"It's beachwear right?" Marlon's lips were slightly curved. "What's a beach without sand? I think it would add an extra touch to the display room. Don't you think?"

Candace couldn't believe she never thought of this. "Yes, it would. That's actually a marvelous idea."

Her statement prompted a chuckle from Marlon. "Well, I like to surprise others with my ingenious ideas now and again." After a few seconds, he asked, "What are you doing later?"

Candace jolted upward, his question seemingly coming from nowhere. "I'll probably be working. I'm really busy these days." Her words were unsure.

"You can't work all the time. You need to have a little fun now and then." Then Marlon's lips twisted, his eyes piercing hers. "A friend of mine owns a bar. Why don't we go?"

"You mean—together?" Candace's eyelashes fluttered rapidly.

A chuckle escaped Marlon. "Why not? I'm good at other things besides work."

For a moment, Candace wanted to give in to his request. She wanted to be spontaneous for once and forget all her responsibilities. But she couldn't. Actions had consequences, and she didn't want one moment of weakness to affect her for the rest of her life.

"I can't," she said, her heart aching as the words came out of her mouth. "We should keep our relationship strictly professional."

Marlon looked at her, his eyes etching her skin. "Is there anything wrong with us becoming friends?"

"If my boss finds out, I'll be in trouble." Candace wasn't lying. Fraternization with clients was strictly prohibited and if she was caught, it could cost her a job. Still, that was not the main reason Candace rejected Marlon's offer. This man had a presence that overwhelmed her, causing reactions to her body, and that scared her.

Marlon tilted his head, a slight smile on his lip. "Well, just don't let her find out."

It was a tempting offer, but Candace had to decline, her mouth twitching as she did so.

Candace was still going over the conversation with Marlon in her head later in the afternoon when her phone rang. "Hello?" she answered without watching the number.

"Candace," her friend Laura spoke in a high-pitched voice with a dragging drawl. This could only mean one thing. She wanted something.

"Whatever it is Laura, the answer is no," Candace said the firm, her fingers flicking through pages as she pressed the phone to her ears with her shoulder.

"But you don't even know what I want yet," her friend whined.

"It doesn't matter," Candace said. "If you need to sway me, then you know it's something I don't want to do, so forget it."

The other woman continued to whine. "But I'm meeting a guy I met on TikTok for the first time tonight and I need a buffer."

Unlike Candace, her friend Laura was extremely outgoing, dating almost every week, usually with different men. Their friendship was unusual - as the women were so different - but they had a common interest. Both women were different from their peers, so they found solace in each other.

"I don't want to end up with a stalker or something," Laura argued.

"Well, here's a tip." Candace held the phone with her hand now. "How about you don't date people you meet on social media?"

"But the men I usually meet in person are so *boring*." The woman's words were so high-pitched that Candace had to pull the phone away from her ears. "I just need my best friend to have my back." Then she said in an almost babyish tone, "What do you say, bestie?"

Candace took in a sharp breath and released it with a force. "Fine. But this is the last time." That were the same words she used the last time Laura forced her into an uncomfortable situation with one of her dates.

"Great. We'll meet at a bar that just opened up at eight. I'll text you the address." And without giving Candace time to change her mind, her friend ended the call.

Candace looked up at the clock on the wall. It was already 6 pm. She'll finish her work and head to the bar right after.

Chapter 3

The bar wasn't like any of the other bars Laura usually dragged Candace to. This one had a dark aura about it, something unnerving but also exciting.

As she walked through the door, she was greeted by a man who scanned her with a suspicious device. It wasn't a metal detector, but he used it in the same way before giving her a blue band. Candace dismissed her concerns. Maybe it was just a new version of the safety tool.

Inside was sectioned into three, the table area for those choosing to eat with their drinks, the bar counter if they are patrons who just wanted to drink, and a VIP section, where apparently only those with red bands were allowed.

Candace navigated through the packed bar, occupying the only available stool at the counter. From there, she scanned the room for her friend, who was apparently late. The sound of glass hitting wood directed her attention behind where the bartender was giving her his full attention.

He was a tall, muscular man with unique green eyes, eyes she only saw once in her life. The man had broad shoulders and a pronounced jawline with large hands. He was definitely one of the most handsome men she ever saw, but rugged.

"I didn't order that," Candace said, referring to the drink the bartender placed in front of her.

"I know," the man said, his lips curling to the side. "This one is on the house." Then he leaned in. "Only for a gorgeous lady like you."

Candace's jaw fell. She had never been complimented for her appearance before and especially not from a man that looked like him. Candace looked up at the man, wanting to trail her fingers in his rugged beard.

"I really shouldn't." She pushed the drink back to him, but he was not about to give in that easily.

"Of course, you can," the man said and offered the drink once again. This time he flashed her a smile, which had Candace thankful she was seated. Otherwise, she would have lost her footing.

She took the glass slowly and said, "Well, thank you for your generosity," before sipping the aqua drink.

The bartender kept his eyes on her. "I'm Paul, by the way."

"I'm Candace."

The man winked at her before leaving to attend to another customer, while Candace quietly finished her drink. By the time her drink had finished, there was another one waiting for her.

"Oh, no - no. I can't accept this." Candace shook her head but couldn't stop the smile from curling her lips. "This is too much." Then she pushed out her lips. "Your boss would be upset if he finds out."

Paul leaned in and whispered, "Then we just won't tell him."

It was strange hearing this phrase again. Candace wrapped her fingers around the glass as she remembered her conversation with Marlon not too long ago.

Noticing her blank stare, Paul continued, "If you don't take it, then I'll have to throw it out and he'll get even more upset. So do us both a favor and just accept the drink, ok?"

"Fine," Candace snapped out of her daze. "But no more ok."

"I can't make any promises," Paul said, walking away before she could speak again.

Maybe Candace should have found out the contents of the drink before consuming two glasses. She had never been able to hold her alcohol, and this time was no different. By the time her friend called her, Candace was already experiencing the effects of her mystery drink.

"So, I've decided not to go on the date after all," Laura began. "Meeting men on the internet is too dangerous and there are so many creeps out there."

"That's what I've been telling you," Candace said with a slur before pushing herself off the stool and heading to the bathroom. Her head spun slightly, and she wobbled slightly, drifting into a busty redhead. Candace apologized with a raised hand before continuing her phone conversation. "But you're still coming to the bar right. I'm already here."

"Uh, I don't think so. This man I met with last week called and he wants to go to a concert. I'm leaving my apartment now."

Candace was in line now, waiting for the person inside the washroom to vacate. "Are you kidding me?" she screamed at her friend over the funky rock song.

"I'm sorry love I'll make it up to you. Get home safe," Laura said before ending the call. Candace fumed as she entered the bathroom after the skinny man left.

She ran into the open stall, her phone still in hand as she bent over the bowl to release the unsettling contents of her stomach. There was no force involved, but Candace clung to the sides of the bowl until her phone slipped from her hand and into the water.

Candace just stood there for a while, with her eyes bulging, watching the device as it sunk to the bottom. In her drunken haze, it was hard to decipher if her phone had actually fallen in, but there was no doubt about her dilemma.

Her first thought was just to abandon it. She could simply get a new phone with the same number the following day. But then she'll have to go through the trouble of reinstalling her contacts and she was expecting a call from Marlon the next morning. What if he called and her phone was not operational as yet? If Sarah found out, then she would be in trouble. And she would just feel empty without her phone.

No. She had to get it back, but that was something easier said than done. Candace couldn't bring her hand to the bowl, no matter how hard she tried. Looking away didn't help. Her lids involuntarily opened.

Feeling beaten and overall exhausted, Candace allowed her body to settle onto the tiled floor with her back to the door, and slowly the world around her disappeared.

Chapter 4

"Hey, Paul," Jake, a friend of the man, said, "we've got a problem in the bathroom. A lady passed out in the stall."

"Dammit," Paul muttered under his breath as he dropped the glass in his hand and headed toward the unisex bathroom. As a bartender for many years, he had seen a lot of things and now that he owned his own bar, he didn't expect things to be any different. Although he was taken aback by the woman on the floor. Straight blonde hair obscured her face, but there was no doubt. It was the woman he gave the drinks to before. But how was she passed out? She only had two drinks.

"Hey. The line outside is backing up. What are you going to do with her?" Jake was standing behind him.

"The same thing we do with all our drunk patrons. Call the last number on her phone." Paul angled himself to get a closer look at the woman, looking a bit erotic even in her sleep.

"That might be a little troublesome, man." Jake pointed to the phone soaking in the bowl. "I'm definitely not getting that."

The bulky man swore under his breath again, considering his option. He definitely couldn't leave her there. He couldn't bring her back to the main bar, either. The VIP room had long couches. She would be comfortable there, but judging by the band on her hand, which was not an option. There was only one place he could bring her.

Paul bent over and lifted the woman into his arms, momentarily taken in by her dazzling eyes. He then brushed past the people waiting in the line outside the washroom and at the back to his private quarters.

The woman didn't even stir, not even when he placed her on the bed and encased her in the covers. Paul took a minute to admire her before returning to deal with the situation she caused in the bathroom. Only after he was able to rejoin his employee behind the bar. Still, his thoughts remained on the woman at the back with her hair scattered about his pillow.

Images of her sultry skin smooth under his touch and her lips, subtle and kissable, teased him. Paul forced his eyes closed and then opened them again while shaking his head. Still, the naughty thoughts swirling around did not disappear. They remained the entire night, even as the bar became emptied as the night winded down.

Paul hesitated for a few seconds before entering the back room he called home. It was a small — a studio apartment—but it was his. He tried his best to turn it into a home, even splurging on the couch set, though he hardly ever used it. Paul was always on the move, organizing for his bar when he wasn't working in it. The little time he spent in his home was spent sleeping or entertaining a female companion.

He took in his guests' appearance once again. She was different from the women he was used to. More conservative, but he found that aspect about her aroused him. Even with her plain white blouse buttoned to the nape of her neck, she caused his manhood to twitch in his pants and his eyes to flicker.

Paul exhaled sharply, turning away from her to get a bottle of water from the refrigerator. He needed to calm himself, but the longer she remained in his presence, the more rattled he became. He needed to get her out of there.

He walked over to her, a determination on his face, shaking her vigorously. "Candace, wake up." The first few times he called, she didn't stir, but finally, she opened her eyes, capturing his green ones. When Paul felt the rise in his crotch, he knew he had to get her out of there before it was too late. This woman didn't travel with his type of crowd. She was innocent, and he wanted to keep it that way.

"Candace. It's late. Is there anyone I could call for you?" His words had an urgency, but Candace's eyes were wild, as if unable to decipher what he was saying. She couldn't possibly still be drunk. Not after two drinks.

"Candace," he said, nudging her shoulder, but his touch only made her eyes wilder.

Oh shit, he thought to himself. *If she keeps looking at me with those big, bulging eyes, I wouldn't be able to contain myself any longer.*

Candace did not know what she was becoming entangled in, yet she reached up to stroke behind Paul's neck and pulled him down for a kiss. She wasn't drunk. The alcohol had long worn out of her system. She was just tired. Tired of always holding herself back, not being able to do what she wanted.

Tired of being too cowardly to take the plunge. Sure, Laura was always getting disappointed by men, but at least she put herself out there. She was not afraid to strive for what she wanted, and Candace admired that. She wanted to be more like Laura and right now she wanted this delicious man with abs of steel.

Paul didn't need further nudging. His body sprawled over her as he clung to her waist, his touch rough but welcoming. Candace shivered under his touch, under the full length of his body and the feel of his hardened dick through his pants.

For a moment, he released her mouth, trailing kisses along her neck, and Candace moaned as he nipped her flesh. No doubt, Paul would make it an unforgettable experience. When his mouth returned to hers, his hands were underneath the hem of her skirt, reaching for her gentle folds. The sensation as his fingers slipped underneath her underwear to rub against her sensitive nub was overwhelming, causing her to wiggle underneath his touch.

"You're so wet," he said, his breathing heavy as he pierced her with intensity. "Come for me." His words were more of a command, which Candace obliged to once the movement of his fingers quickened. She held onto the bed, clutching it tightly as her body convulsed around his fingers, leaving her breathless.

Candace's legs were numb, but Paul was not finished with her. In fact, he was just getting started.

When he tugged at his shirt, buttons scattered about the floor, and the act seemed to create urgency in him. His pants were next and Candace gasped as his manhood sprung free, void of any underwear.

"It's not too late to change your mind," he said, comfortable in his nakedness. Candace couldn't speak. The most she could do was shake her head and the sexy man rid her of her clothing.

He didn't resume his position then. Instead, he flipped Candace over so her stomach rested on the bed, holstering her ass high. A sharp hand came down on her, causing her to cry out, but her cries were not completely out of pain. Candace realized she loved the feeling of being spanked and she loved it, even more, when Paul gripped her by the waist and entered her from the back.

With one fluid movement, he was inside her, cock twitching from her tightness. When he frowned, he aroused her even more, and Candace relaxed, allowing his manhood to better fill her up.

Like his entry, Paul's thrust was far from delicate. It was rough and sharp, pleasurable torture that caused her to scream with every movement. With his hand in her hair, Candace closed her eyes and pushed back on him, matching his intensity. Matching him stroke for stroke as he brought her to new heights.

Candace didn't believe it was possible for her to orgasm twice. None of her previous lovers had accomplished the task. Yet, there she was, convulsing around Paul for the second time for the night. It was absolutely intoxicating, and Candace bucked, clutching the sheet until her knuckles turned white.

When Paul finally exploded in her, there was a force behind it and his fingers dug into her flesh. With a powerful grown, he emptied himself inside her, pushing even deeper until she felt him at her stomach.

Candace had never had sex like this before, and she wanted more.

Chapter 5

Candace's eyes fluttered open as memories of the night played through her mind. It was her intention to be impulsive, but maybe she was too impulsive. Had she really slept with a complete stranger? She peeked at herself, naked underneath the coverings. Then she tilted her head upwards to stare at the man whose chest was bare and legs dangled from underneath the sheet. She had definitely had sex with the sexy bartender. Candace flinched and clamped down on her lips.

What was she going to do?

There was only one thing she could think of. Make a speedy escape before he woke up.

Easing herself out of bed, Candace left her companion with the covers, too afraid to take them away from him. She skipped across the room, retrieving pieces of clothing from where they discarded them the night before, putting each piece on one at a time.

After Candace finished dressing, she looked back at the naked man. He was still asleep, giving her time to ease out of the small accommodation, softly closing the door behind her. When she was out of Paul's apartment, she breathed a sigh of relief and placed her hand on her chest.

Candace picked up the pace now, strutting her legs as she navigated between the tables and chairs stacked on top of them. She was in such a hurry that she didn't notice the huge bulk in front of her, bumping it to him with a force that sent her backward.

That appeared to become a trend.

Candace clutched her forehead - the area smacked by the man even bulkier than Paul - and rubbed hard.

"Watch it," the man said in a rough, rumbling voice, but there was a menacing look in his eyes. It made Candace shiver, but not in the same way Paul did. With this man, Candace wanted to cuddle up and hide.

"Sorry," she said, keeping her head low as she bypassed him and practically ran out of the building.

Outside, she was able to slow her breath and regain her composure. Candace took a few deep breaths and spoke to herself. "You're ok. It's fine. You never have to set foot in that place again."

Her ramblings were meant to reassure her, but they weren't very effective. Candace was still taken aback by the entire situation and shocked at herself.

As soon as her legs were steady enough to walk, Candace went to her apartment. It was not much different from Paul's as it was also a studio. However, hers was exquisitely furnished and had a feminine touch.

When Candace walked into her home, she walked into the sitting room. Here she had placed three couch sets, angled in a semicircle. They hovered around the space saver, which housed the television and the stereo. Candace kept a table with a small fish tank in the corner. She wanted a bigger one with more fish, but Beta fishes are known to be aggressive with other fishes. So she kept Sarah all by herself.

There was a protrusion to the left side of the house where her tiny kitchen stored everything she needed. Everything meant coffee. Since Candace was always working, she seldom spent time at her apartment and therefore rarely cooked. The kitchen shared space with the dining room, which meant Candace only had room for a two-seat set. This wasn't a problem for her since she rarely had a guest over.

Leading from the kitchen was a short walkway that extended into the bed area. With her full-sized bed in the middle, the area was almost filled. This was a sacrifice Candace was willing to make. She needed to have comfortable sleep, but what she didn't need was a lot of closet space.

Much to her friend's dismay, Candace kept her wardrobe simple, focused on plain and neutral-colored clothing with simple designs. Laura had tried multiple times to extend Candace's range, but she was unsuccessful each time. Candace simply tucked away all the clothing her friend bought her into the back of the dresser drawer.

The first thing Candace did after entering the apartment was to take a bath. She felt dirty and uneasy about her night activities and, therefore, drenched herself underneath the shower, letting the water run all over her body, soothing her nerves. Then she wrapped her blonde hair into a neat ponytail and clothed herself in blue jeans and a simple tank top with a gray hoodie. Candace grabbed an apple out of the fridge.

It was a Saturday, and she didn't have to work but had organized a meet-up with Marlon so he could show her his plans. On the way to the office she bought a hot cup of coffee, black, then strolled into the office with bags under her eyes and a scrunched-up face.

"Long night?" Marlon asked, his hands immediately pulling out the chair for her to sit.

"Extremely," Candace said, taking a sip of her drink while sitting on the chair. "I feel like I've been run over by a truck."

"Well, I'll make this short so you can go home and get some rest." Marlon spread his plans on the table in the conference room. "Ok, so this is what I have so far. If you agree with everything here, then I will go into more details."

Candace pushed forward in her chair, analyzing the drawings of the details they had gone through before. The entire time, Marlon sat watching her, with his lips curved into a gentle smile.

Suddenly, she felt self-conscious. "What is it?"

He shook his head. "Nothing. I just like watching beautiful things."

Candace's eyes widened at his words. Did that mean she was beautiful? She had never been told she was beautiful by a man before. Not even those she had slept with.

"Stop joking," she chuckled and tapped his arms. "I'm plain."

Marlon looked deeply into her eyes. "Sometimes plain is better. Like vanilla ice cream." He reached out and touched her arm. "And I love vanilla ice cream."

When Marlon touched her, Candace's heart started to escalate, but not the same way it did when she was with Paul. With Paul, it was mostly lust, a feral attraction to a very sexy man, but with Marlon, it was much more, an inner connection, entangling their souls. Both men were completely different, and she felt differently about them. With Paul, she wanted to screw hard, but with Marlon; she wanted to make love and cuddle.

Still, what kept her from accepting Marlon's offer was still an issue. He was related to work and, therefore, untouchable.

Candace pulled her hand from his reach, and the moment she did, she felt an emptiness. "You incorporated my suggestions beautifully. I have no alterations to this design."

What else did she expect? With Marlon, it felt like they were in sync, knowing exactly what the other wanted. If that was true, then he must feel what she felt every time they were close to each other.

"How about dinner?" Marlon leaned in, his eyes wide.

"You know I can't do that," she responded, putting her bag on her shoulder.

"What's wrong with grabbing a bite after work?" Marlon's head was tilted. "Aren't co-workers allowed to eat together?"

Candace eyed Marlon for a long time. Despite everything, she wanted to spend more time with him. Last night, she broke the rules and had sex with a sexy stranger. Why not bend the rules some more?

"Just dinner?" she asked, her eyes wide as her head jerked backward.

"Just dinner," he said, his hands against his chest. In his mind, he was saying, today dinner, tomorrow something else.

Chapter 6

"Do you have any place in mind?" Marlon asked, but Candace kept her lips sealed and shook her head.

She couldn't tell him the last time she went out to a restaurant was before her boyfriend brutally dumped her for another woman. That was two years ago and since then she hadn't been with anyone, except for the sexy bartender.

"That's alright." Then he snapped his fingers. "I think I know the perfect place. Do you like Mediterranean food?"

Candace's face lit up, and she felt energized. "It's actually my favorite."

"Then you would love this place." Marlon grabbed her hand, and his touch made her flinch. She loved it. "Come on."

Marlon took Candace to a cozy restaurant, fifteen minutes onto an isolated road. And like a gentleman, he opened the door for her to get out of the car.

"Look at that," Candace said, her head upward into the night sky. "There are so many stars. It's beautiful."

"The scenery is one of the things I like most about this restaurant," Marlon said, leading her to the balcony. "When you taste the food, you will understand the second."

It was a magnificent restaurant with low lighting and a simple yet intricate setting. The theme was natural and earthy, with the fresh mountain air enriching the patrons.

Marlon guided Candace to a seat on the balcony, holding the chair out for her. "How did you find this place?"

He sat down opposite her as she scanned the surrounding trees and the fireflies that darted through them. "A friend of mine owns it."

"Not all of it." Candace and Marlon both turned their heads to the dark-haired man as he approached. "Marlon," he said to his friend. "I haven't seen you in a while. Came to check on your investment?"

Marlon greeted his friend and then introduced Candace. "Henry is the owner of the restaurant and the best chef there is."

"Come on, man. You don't have to say that." Then Henry turned to Candace with a grin on his face. She couldn't quite decipher it, but there was meaning there. "But he's right. I am."

"Oh, so modest." Marlon's sarcasm was obvious. "Just treat us good tonight, OK?"

"Don't I always?" Henry raised his eyebrows. Before he left the table. "Don't worry, I'll make it a meal you can't forget."

It was hard not to smile in such a magnificent place. "You guys seem close," she said, referring to Henry and Marlon.

"Yes, we are," he responded. 'It's a bunch of us, actually. We grew up together and remained friends."

Candace couldn't imagine having that many friends. "That must be nice. I didn't have many friends going up. Nobody wanted to hang out with the weird one."

"Well, it's their loss." Marlon held her gaze. "Because you are an absolutely wonderful person."

Candace smiled, her eyes sparkling under the crescent moonlight. "You barely know me."

"I know enough to realize that you are a caring, intelligent, and heartwarming person. There is a quiet nature about you, but I can sense that you're far from quiet when your loved ones are involved." Candace tilted her head, her forehead scrunched and mouth slightly open as Marlon continued. "I've been interested in you since the first time I saw you. Of course, I've been paying attention."

Her words caught in her throat, and it took a while to get them out. When she did, every word sounded like a surprise. "You're interested in me?"

"Wasn't it obvious?" Marlon straightened himself. "Well, let me make it clear so that there is no confusion." He took her hand, causing a surge to run through her body. "I like you, Candace. A lot. And not as a friend. I wouldn't always be working with your company and I hope when that day comes, you'll allow me to be a part of your life."

Candace couldn't believe it. A week ago, she didn't think the opposite sex noticed her. Now here she was with a handsome man as he confessed his love for her.

"You don't have to say anything now. Let's just enjoy our time together." Marlon was an accurate representation of a gentleman, and the more time she spent with him, Candace was finding it harder to reject him. She held his gaze, her lips parting to speak, but then they were interrupted.

"Shrimp linguini for the man and my special zucchini lasagna for the lady. Bon appetite." Henry served them and turned left right away, sensing he was disturbing something. He had that connection with Marlon to sense his emotions. And at that moment, Marlon's emotions were intense.

After Henry left, Marlon changed the subject, focusing more on Candace's pleasurable pastimes. He found out she loved to read and watch Asian dramas even though she didn't speak any of the Asian languages. He told her about his childhood and traveling around the world and she laughed heartedly as he relayed his experience in the Amazon rainforest.

"I swear I thought I would die." The smile was in his eyes.

Candace had forgotten all her troubles, sinking into the magical night. "So, what did you do?"

"I dropped my stuff and hot-tailed it out of there as fast as I could." Marlon used his hands to display his fast motion. "I don't mess with anacondas. That's where I draw the line."

Candace held her stomach. She was laughing so hard that it was hard for her to maintain her composure. When she finally settled down, she said. "This is the most fun I've had in a long time."

Her words caused Marlon to straighten his face. "It doesn't have to end right now." He held her gaze. "How about we go to one more place tonight?"

Before, Candace would have objected. She would have made some excuse to reject Marlon's suggestion, but now that she had gotten to know him a lot better, there was only one thing to say. "Sure."

Chapter 7

Candace followed Marlon as he walked down the street, making a sudden stop as he slowed in front of the building.

"Is this where you want to go?" Her eyes dart up towards the sign, a sign she barely glimpsed when she sprinted away earlier that morning.

"It is," Marlon said, and then turned his body to get a better view of her, flinching as he noticed her growing paler. Marlon went forward and took her hand, his face stern and encouraging. "I'll be with you the entire time."

Candace took a step back, but something prevented her from completely retreating. She did not want Marlon to know what happened there the night before, but the look in Marlon's eyes reassured her everything was going to be fine.

Marlon held her hand and guided her into the bar just as the last group of patrons left.

Candace was hoping there would be other people and she could somehow blend into the crowd, but with the place empty, Paul's eyes fell on her easily.

Marlon made introductions. "Paul. This is the woman I was telling you about. Her name is—"

"Candace," Paul said, keeping his eyes on the woman that left his bed early in the morning. "We've met."

Candace turned away her head just as the two men shared a look.

"Candace, this is my bud, Paul. He owns this bar."

She tried to speak, but as hard as she tried, no sound came out, so she forced a smile and nodded instead.

Then Paul took her hand, his free one gently brushing the hair behind her ears. "Candace it's ok. Paul is irresistible to women. I understand."

Paul came closer to them, a smirk on his face and drinks in his hands. He shared it among the three and Candace reluctantly drank. By the time she was halfway through the glass, the effects of the alcohol were already prevalent. She was more relaxed and laughing at the duo's jokes. Just like Marlon, Paul had many interesting stories to tell. Stories she would have heard if she stuck around after they had sex.

"So, which one of us do you like more?" The question was unexpected, and Paul's expression told Candace he was serious.

She couldn't answer. Paul was tough and exciting, whereas Marlon was compassionate and gentle. They each had the qualities the others lacked. How did these two men become friends? Candace's eyes were building now, her heart beating fast, until Marlon leaned over and placed his mouth on her lips. His kiss was gentle, and it renewed her spirit. She returned his kiss, closing her eyes in the moment. When Marlon pulled away, he said. "If you can't decide, you don't have to choose."

Candace tilted her head in confusion. What did Marlon mean by that? She didn't get to ask as Paul soon answered her. His act was similar to Marlon's but his kiss was much more domineering.

A concession of blinks followed as Candace tried to get a grasp on the situation.

"You could have us both if you want," Paul said, right before he placed another kiss on her lips. He deepened it, lifting her into his arms and carrying her away. Candace latched onto him, her feet around his waist.

Paul's release of her body onto the bed was far from gentle, but Marlon balanced his aggressiveness. He towered over her now, caressing every part of her body before his hand slid underneath her dress.

When he touched her, Candace's eyes rolled back, and she clung to the sheet. She was enjoying the intense sensation that came with Marlon's advances, and then he was gone. In his place, Paul removed the rest of her clothing, nipping her lip the entire time.

Not until he settled between her thighs, did she notice he was naked, sexy in all his glory. Candace held on firmly to his waist as he entered her, much like the night before, quickly placing her in a seductive trance. She latched on to his back, digging her nails into his flesh, an act that didn't seem to phase him. When his movements became more rapid, Candace knew he was close to his end and aided him.

Breathless, Paul withdrew and Marlon filled his place, but he didn't enter her. He pulled Candace on top of him and kissed her passionately, brushing her cheeks gently with the tips of his finger. And so, the hectic atmosphere had turned docile.

Marlon and Candace clung together until she grew restless. She wanted him, all of him, so Candace ignored all her previous concerns and eased onto him, gyrating back and forth as she did. Their rotations were slow and systematic, every inch of them shivering with passion. When Candace fell from her height, she took Marlon down with her and the two clung together, eventually falling asleep in each other's arms.

Chapter 8

Candace woke to whispered voices in the arms of one of her lovers. She looked to Marlon. His lips curved into a gentle smile as he slept, but Paul was not in the apartment.

At first, she settled into Marlon's arms, but something was gnawing at her. The voices were aggressive, and Paul's absence left her on edge.

She followed the voices as they led her to the bar, which was occupied by three bulky men. Paul was one of them, and he flinched as she approached.

"I did not realize that your taste in women has changed." Candace's eyes followed the words to a recognizable face. It was the man she ran into the night before. But it wasn't him who spoke. It was the skinnier one standing next to him. "I didn't realize you were into humans now?"

Human? What did he mean by that?

Candace found his comment strange but dismissed it as a misunderstanding. It had to be some inside joke implying Paul was a beast. After having sex with him twice, she could see how something like that could stick to him.

"I told you he had a human in here," the other one said to his companion, then directed his words to Paul. "You know better than to hoard the tributes. We share all with our tribe."

"You are mistaken." Paul's hand was folded into a fist, leaving the veins on his arms visible. "She is no tribute."

The men were staring at her now as if she was the only morsel in the lion's den. It made her uncomfortable, and she folded her arms and shifted her weight on one leg.

"Isn't she for the tribe?" The skinnier man's eyebrows were lifted, and he seem baffled that Paul was not offering her to them.

What was she anyway, some kind of object that could be tossed around and given away? Why were they speaking about her as if she had no authority over where she needed to be?

"I am not going anywhere with you, so you can get that silly thought out of your head." Candace suddenly felt invincible.

The bigger man laughed. "You seem to think that you have a choice in the matter." Then he became more serious. "Human mates are property of the tribe."

"I am no one's property," Candace shouted, placing her hands on her hips.

The bulky man laughed, and the other one narrowed his gaze at her. "You will return with us to our den, whether you like it or not." His gaze was intense, and it made her shiver.

"She's not going anywhere with you." Candace did not realize Marlon had entered the room. He walked in further, his eyes glowing green as he passed her. "I thought we made it clear that we are no longer part of the tribe."

"What do you feel this is? You can't just leave as you want. Our blood is not so easily discarded." The tension in the air was thick with the two intruders displaying as much aggression as her lovers. Still, Candace couldn't understand most of what they were saying.

"We're done following the bidding of the tribe blindly." Paul's veins were bulging now, and they also appeared to be pulsing. "From now on, we're following our own rules."

Paul's mysterious nighttime guest's hands were large, but at that moment they seemed larger. Unusually so. It looked as if it was outweighing his body.

Candace took a good look at the men. Both of them looked out of proportion, swelling on the face and the upper body. Taking a step backward, she looked at Marlon and Paul to realize that they had taken on a similar appearance.

The four men's bodies warped in and out of shape until they discarded their clothes and their human forms. Long nose replaced their short ones, and their eyes appeared more animalistic. Even the unique green eyes of her lovers adapted to their bodies' change, glowing in the darkness.

Candace's hand was clamped onto her mouth as she took in the full extent of their transformation: pointed ears, a protruding nose, large paws, fur, and hind legs. There was no doubt in her mind that these men were wolves.

No. Werewolves.

Candace shrieked as the biggest of them all leaped into the air and targeted the gray wolf, still trailing a piece of Paul's clothing. Based on its size, one hit from this wolf could cause serious injury. Luckily, it was slow, giving Paul enough time to jump out of the way and maneuver into an attack of his own.

Paul's wolf was swift, but not as much as Marlon's who battled the last wolf. They attacked each other with their paws, slashing across each other's faces and leaping into the air.

Tables and chairs tumbled to the floor as the fight escalated, leaving Candace shivering in the corner of the room. She had no idea what to do in that situation. Should she run or stay? Call the police or leave them to settle it?

They were, after all, wolves. Would they even want the police involved?

In the end, Candace did nothing, her body unable to coordinate, especially with her indecisive thoughts. Instead, she squeezed herself into the corner and waited until the commotion ended. Until both Marlon had his opponent pinned down and Paul's was knocked out on the floor. Only then she could breathe again, but now she had a new problem. With the adrenaline rush normalizing, her brain now had time to accept what had happened.

She had two lovers, who were friends, and both turned into wolves. Not only this, but two other wolves were trying to claim her. It was an unbelievable reality, and its acceptance sent her into darkness.

Chapter 9

"Ugh." The sound spilled out of Candace's mouth before she opened her eyes. Pressing her hand against her forehead, she tried to ease herself off the bed.

A hand rested firmly on her shoulders, pushing her back down. "Take it easy. You were out of it for a while."

Candace forced herself to focus on the figure hovering above her, taking in his shrunken eyes and twisted mouth.

"Marlon," she whispered through dry lips. "I had the weirdest dream."

"Did you?" he asked before easing himself away. When Marlon returned, there was a glass of water in her hand and he clung to it while he assisted her in drinking. Then he settled her back in bed, snuggling her with the sheets. Finally, he released a heavy sigh but said nothing.

Still, Candace's dream disturbed her, and she felt the need to speak about it. "I dreamed that you, Paul, and two other men changed into wolves and had a big fight in the bar." She chuckled. "Isn't that ridiculous?"

Marlon looked at Paul, and the two exchanged a look before he tucked Candace in the sheet again, although nothing was out of place.

"Candace," Marlon said so softly she almost didn't hear him. "That was not a dream." He gave her a few seconds to digest the statement as Paul watched their interaction from across the room, leaning against the wall.

Candace's thoughts were still in shambles, so she believed she misheard him. "What?" She rubbed her temples in a circular motion to tried and relieve to pain in her head.

Marlon took a deep breath and released it. "Paul and I are werewolves. What you saw wasn't a dream. We really did turn into wolves."

Candace's eyes bulged and her jaw dropped slightly right before her lips began to quiver.

"You have nothing to fear. Paul and I will never hurt you." He paused. "We don't hurt anyone."

"And those guys," she stammered, her hand clutching the sheet.

"They are also werewolves." He took a deep breath and then went on to explain further. "Werewolves are pack creatures. We do and share everything."

"And follow our clan leader blindly," Paul said for the first time since Candace woke up. He said the words with so much scorn, like it was the thing he hated most in the world.

"That we do," Marlon agreed. "Or at least we used to. Paul and I grew tired of being someone's puppet and decided to leave the clan. The leader respected our decision. He doesn't want to force that life on anyone who doesn't want it. But some of the other members are not so understanding."

"We sent them back with their tail between their legs though," Paul joked, a smile plastered across his face.

Marlon took back control in explaining the situation the best he could, so as to not frighten Candace. "And don't worry. They won't bother us again. If they acted without the leader's consent - which I think they did - they would be punished for it."

"So they're gone?" she asked, her eyes searching the room.

"Yes. You don't have to worry about them," Marlon reassured her, cautiously tapping her hand. When he was confident enough, she wouldn't flinch from his touch, he took her hand in his completely, gently stroking it.

"What were those guys talking about when they mentioned tribute?" Candace was still a bit confused and while she had them in the explaining mood, she wanted to get as much information as she could.

"As a rule in our clan, if one of us takes a human mate, we are obligated to share her with the clan. You see, unlike humans, we have many mates." Marlon tapped her hand. "You don't have to be concerned about that. We will never share you with any of them."

Candace sighed, a soft smile framing her lips. "So what now?" she asked, looking from one man to the other.

"Well, that is completely up to you. You need to decide if you want to be part of our world or not," Paul said, his hand folded loosely across his chest. It was hard to determine how anxious he felt. Only his tightly pressed lips gave it away.

Candace hesitated. "Well, I don't know." She looked at both men. "Paul, you're tough and aggressively sexy and Marlon, you're compassionate and passionate. I have feelings for both of you." She lowered her head. "I'm sorry. I don't know who to choose."

"Who said you have to choose?" Marlon's words caused her head to rise again. "Did you not hear me say we share our human mates? Paul and I may not be in the clan anymore, but we are still brothers of the wolf. There are certain rules we still follow. What we want to know from you is if you would accept us as your mates. Do you object to being with werewolves?"

Candace didn't know how to answer that. Never in her years did she imagine having such a question thrown at her, so she didn't answer. At least not with words at first. She reached over and pressed her lips to Marlon's, noticing the immediate rise in his pants. When she pulled away, she said, "I don't think I can be with werewolves." Then a smile broadened across her face. "Luckily, to me, you guys are just Marlon and Paul, and my love for you will never fade."

THE END